HOT WIFE SUMMER

A FILTHY DIRTY SUMMER

FRANKIE LOVE

ABOUT

HOT WIFE SUMMER
A Filthy Dirty Summer
By Frankie Love

She's a Certified W.I.L.F.

When I see Baylee at the bar, looking hot as hell, I
want to approach her. Ask her out.
Bring her to bed.
Then I see a wedding ring on her finger.
I've never so badly wanted a woman I couldn't have.
Then I see her approached by a man who pulls her
outside and shoves her in the trunk of a car.
I don't know who this asshole is, but I won't let him
touch her like that. She may belong to another man —
but she needs a protector.

I go into beast mode and that's when sh*t gets real crazy.

It's a hot summer night, and there's a wife I'd like to f*ck.

First, I need to save her. Then, I'll make her mine.

****DO NOT WORRY!!!! THERE IS NO CHEATING IN THIS TWISTED LIL MOTORCYCLE CLUB FANTASY. I PROMISE! READ IT TO FIND OUT HOW BLAZE ENDS UP WITH BAYLEE, HIS ONE TRUE LOVE!**

Welcome to a filthy dirty summer! Drop it like it's hot with your 17 favorite instalove authors! Each stand-alone story delivers a scorching, fantasy-fueled romance! No need to pack a swimsuit—your kindle is all you need for a wet and wild summer!

1

BLAZE

DAMN, the club is packed. It's a hot June night if there ever was one. I'm thirty years old, and I swear this might be the hottest summer on record.

"Why are we being glorified bouncers, of all things?" Capone asks as we make our rounds through the club.

"We're keeping the peace, Capone. A lot of drunks, a lot of macho egos, things can spiral out of control quickly. We aren't in the business of anyone getting hurt. Unless they should be hurt, anyway."

"This is so dull. If we need bouncers we should just hire people."

Capone's a new prospect for the Motorcycle Club. We got him out of a pretty rough group in the city. He's trying to get on a better path in his life, and the club president thought our brotherhood would be the way to help him.

"Take pride in being a protector. It's one of the most manly things a guy can do."

He has scars on his cheeks. A childhood accident. Everyone has a nickname around these parts, a title of affection and something to bring us closer. It would have been obvious to call him Scarface, but our club's president is named Scar already and that might have been a tad confusing. So we named him after the original, Al Capone. He likes it, and it's growing on me as well.

I have to agree with him that this is kind of dull, however. I wouldn't snub my duty to the club, and I do it proudly, but I can't deny that the luster is gone. The past decade at the Wildfire MC clubhouse has been full of great memories and I wouldn't trade them for anything, but I'm growing to realize a man is more than the bond with his brothers.

Hot summer nights like this one make me remember my childhood, when I was home from school. Running the fields, being taught to shoot by my dad during the weekdays and hunting on the weekends. The entire family would come together around the grill, hell, I even miss the Kool-Aid my mother used to make. Times were tough then, but I'm missing it all the same.

Memories of my blood family. Memories of things I

haven't had in years. Not since the accident and the cancer, a one-two punch of the world's cruelty. I can't complain too much as life hasn't been too bad to me outside that, but damn, that was a blow.

A half-drunk beer in hand, I continue my rounds, making sure everything is under control, and making sure Capone pays attention. The bar is simultaneously our clubhouse and our business, so we have a lot of people around town come in for drinks. As one of the few social places in this small town, young men and women come in looking for love.

Or something like it, anyway. Lot of these folks are just bored, and entertaining one another with their bodies is as good an entertainment as anything else. More power to them if that's what they enjoy. That's just not me.

I need a woman, but unlike a lot of the guys I see coming in here, I have standards. The woman who will be my queen and the mother of my children can't just be any girl who walks through that door. Sure, I notice the cute girls here, but looks aren't everything. If my folks taught me anything, it's that you need a spark to build the foundation of a good family, and I'm not going to settle just because I'm not a twenty-something anymore.

Most of the women here are attractive enough, but they've been to the bar enough for me to know them. They aren't for me. None of them are. I never expected love to come walking through the front door. But, then, the world's got a way of taking you by surprise when you least expect it, doesn't it?

As Capone and I reach the bar proper, I see an unfamiliar but gorgeous face.

She's sitting on a stool, looking petite, a white tank top on. It's a tad too big for her, but her curves shine right on through anyway and give me a bit of a look at her perky chest. Tight jeans show off the rest of her and I have to say that I like everything I'm seeing. She turns her head, looking nervous as hell for some reason, but it's enough for me to realize she's the hottest thing on the planet.

I want her so damn bad.

I don't know what it is — nobody has this kind of effect on me — but just looking at her, I know I want her to be mine.

"Who are you looking at, Blaze?" Capone asks.

"The most beautiful woman in the world."

"Her? Yeah, good luck, old man," he laughs. He takes out his phone and starts doing whatever kids his age do on those things.

The object of my fascination raises a glass to her lips, and my heart immediately comes crashing down into my gut. There's a diamond ring on her finger. And a big one too. Someone's already claimed her. Goddammit. How can the universe be this cruel?

Despite the hurdle of her already being in a

committed relationship, I can't help but keep on looking her way. She's the type of girl who is just damn captivating, and the unselfconsciousness of her movements tells me that she doesn't know it. I want to show her how special she is but the code of the Wildfire MC doesn't tolerate any homewreckers.

Not that I'd want to do that... but she makes it a tempting proposition.

I look but don't touch for what feels like forever and also not nearly long enough. I push Capone through the motions, patrolling the bar, but always keeping an eye on her. She seems to be alone, which confuses me. A married woman showing up at a bar like this alone indicates that her life might not be all sunshine and rainbows. The desire to go be her knight in shining armor is pretty strong, which surprises me. I'm not the kind of guy who'd normally be full-on pining for a wife I can't have.

A wife I wish was mine, crazy as it sounds.

I'm trying to forget her, go about my business, when I hear a commotion at the bar. Some schmuck is grabbing at her and I instantly see red.

He's in a leather jacket, but he's not one of ours and there's no tags to suggest that he's part of any other MC. He's kind of scrawny and rough, looking about three times her age and like he hasn't seen the inside of a gym any time during his life.

He yanks her right to her feet. The utter terror in

her eyes suggests that this isn't some playful rough-housing. They share some words, but over the chaos of the club I can't hear anything they're saying. He's pissed, she's scared, and he starts dragging her off. Her father, maybe?

I shift nervously. I'm not one to pick fights, but I'm sure as hell not going to stand idly by either. I keep my distance but follow them, itching to jump in if I see something that tells me I should punch this guy.

Because more than anything, that's what I want to do.

2

BAYLEE

THE WILDFIRE MOTORCYCLE CLUB is a bit farther out than I usually go, but I wanted out of the house more than anything tonight, and I didn't want to be found either.

My whole life I have felt trapped and deep down I am just longing to be free ... to be loved.

My usual haunt for when I want to get far away from home is Joe's Tavern, much closer to where I live. But my dad and Uncle Jericho's first guess would be to look for me there, so that meant it was off the table.

I don't even like drinking that much, but one beer I can nurse for a few hours is cheaper than what I'd need to pay to justify hiding out somewhere else, like at a restaurant. Plus I can people-watch at a bar.

Wildfire turned out to be pretty good for that. It could get pretty wild, people dancing, shouting, and a fist fight even broke out earlier in the night. Both participants wound up at the end of the bar with arms over each other's shoulders, mugs in hand, the bartender happily filling them back up all night. Drunk as heck is preferable to fighting, I suppose.

My little runaway stunts like tonight have been getting more and more frequent. I guess I can't call it running away anymore, but my father would disagree. The bartender doesn't care that I'm twenty years old, and Dad doesn't care either. Dad still acts like he owns me. Like I am an asset to him, someone who has to earn her keep. If I don't? He'll make me regret it.

Tonight I just had to get away. It's the anniversary of my mother's death. It always makes him more ornery and violent. On nights like tonight, I make sure to be far away, as the last thing I want is to be there to find out what stupid thing he did next.

Long term? I don't know what to do. Small towns like this aren't exactly rife with opportunities. And I need money to leave, but the tips I get from being a part-time waitress aren't going to get me to a bigger city.

I'm sitting at the bar, running a finger over my glass and wondering just how long I can sit here without ordering another, when a hand closes around my arm.

"There you are, you ungrateful little bitch." My uncle's voice sends a chill down my spine and he yanks my hand away from the glass, which wobbles but doesn't fall over.

"Uncle Jericho, what are you doing here?" I snap back, rising to my feet.

"You think you can run away like this? Your father is looking for you."

"How did you find me?"

"He has eyes everywhere, little girl."

I seethe, but a place like this probably has enough scummy people who would rat me out, and my father had no shortage of 'friends.'

"I'm not going anywhere, Uncle Jericho. I'm twenty, I'm an adult."

"You're his daughter, and no number is going to change that."

"No!"

My plea falls on deaf ears as he pulls me along. I am not strong enough to fight back against him, so he's giving me the option of walking or being dragged along the ground. Having some dignity, I choose the former. As he pulls me toward the door, I glance around at the crowd, hoping that one of these men will stop this madness, see that I definitely don't want to go with Uncle Jericho and step in.

In my panic, I see him.

Sharp blue eyes staring my way, thick stubble, brownish red hair, all muscle. He's a biker, an actual biker, not just a wannabe like Uncle Jericho. He has patches on his jacket and everything. And he's looking right at me. Despite the peril of my situation, I feel butterflies flutter in my belly. Of all the times to develop a crush.

"Where are we going?" I demand of my uncle. "Dad can't want me home this bad just so he can yell at me."

"We got something special planned for tonight, girlie. You're going to love it."

I bite my lip as we get out to Uncle Jericho's beater of a car. He throws open the back door and shoves me in. I contemplate just sliding across the seat, escaping out the other side and running for it, but I know that I could also be riding home in the trunk if I antagonize Uncle Jericho too much.

He gets in the front seat and the car rumbles out onto the highway. The terror inside me is so strong, so potent. I don't know what Uncle Jericho meant by something special. It doesn't take a rocket scientist to know that I'm not really going to love it, whatever it is.

I look out the back window, imagining a life where I was able to save up enough money to get away from here. Away from my dad and uncle. And I see a single headlight shining right back at me.

Is... is that the hot biker I saw before? Is he following me?

Could I really be so lucky, that he saw me and is coming to my rescue?

3

———

BLAZE

On the surface? I guess I could have written it off as an angry father being overly controlling of his daughter. My gut tells me it doesn't smell right though. "Capone, you got this, just make sure those two idiots don't start punching one another again."

"Sure, man, whatever." He rolls his eyes. I just gotta have faith something will get through to that boy, because I have somewhere else to be right now.

I head out to the garage where our bikes rest, saying goodbye to the guy playing bouncer outside the bar. "Heading out, Echo."

Echo cocks an eyebrow. "What's eating you, Blaze? You aren't normally the evening joyride type of guy."

"I'm still not, I'm just seeing something I shouldn't be seeing."

He grumbles. "That girl that just came through

here? Yeah, I didn't like the looks of that either. Make sure you give me a call if you need backup, man."

I climb onto my hog just as that shitty sedan pulls out of the parking lot. They got a bit of a head start but it isn't ground that my girl can't make up.

Speaking of girls, her eyes haunt me. As they locked with mine while she was being pulled from the bar, I could see she's terrified of what's happening to her. If this was your typical controlling spouse or father, she wouldn't be this spooked.

I guess it's all still just a hunch, though, and I'll be answering to Scar if I just wantonly start throwing fists at bar patrons unprovoked.

So I need to know more. I tail the sedan, and see her peer out the back, giving me sad puppy dog eyes. It is heartbreaking to see on a woman who I only wanted to see smile.

Our path takes us to the outskirts of town, deep into the industrial district, the part full of derelict buildings that haven't seen workers for over a decade. A collection of cars is gathered around, and lots of men are about. Some of them are in suits, looking like they got lost on their way home from their Wall Street meetings, others looking like the same roughneck brand of guy that I am. Some are in their early twenties, and the ages spread out from there, including some guy who can't be less than eighty.

The only girls?

Young. Barely legal, clearly being preyed upon for their youth alone. All of them are in dresses that barely go past their thighs. More importantly, all of them look absolutely terrified, some of them with tears rolling down their cheeks. I don't think their consent is being considered in whatever this is.

Interspersed with the scumbag guys are guys who are packing, in varying degrees of openness. Some just have pieces on their legs, others are carrying rifles. "Security," as they probably claim to be.

My damsel in distress is pulled out of the back of the sedan by the same scumbag from before. She's yelled at by another man, who shoves a dress into her chest — skimpy and similar to what the other girls are wearing. He pulls at her shirt, and I piece together that he wants her to change out here and right now, with the eyes of a dozen horny men looking her up and down.

I watch from a distance, itching to act. She turns as they bear down on her, a futile attempt at modesty. She sees me in the distance, the only one who's spotted me, her doe-like eyes meeting mine as she deals with the shoves and handsiness of the men around her. She mouths a word toward me, and my heart breaks.

Help. She's asking for help.

I feel powerless. I want to charge in, draw my own gun, and start firing wildly at each and every one of those sad excuses for manhood.

But I know better. All that would happen is I'd gain a few dozen new holes and she'd still be in whatever predicament that is about to befall her.

She's not the only one who needs help, but at least I know that help will be coming up right behind me. All it takes is one phone call. "Echo? Yeah, I'm going to need you and everyone else the club can spare."

4

BAYLEE

I'D HEARD Uncle Jericho and my dad talking about things like this, as crassly as they always did.

A 'virgin auction.'

I shuddered at the thought of it. It's such a disgusting idea, and I worried that they would try to make me go to one. I thought that maybe, just maybe, they wouldn't be that horrible to their own blood. Or maybe they thought I was already a whore, sleeping around with any guy who would have me. But they know nothing about me. I am a virgin, and I don't want to give anything to a man who would think I have a price.tag

"You don't even know if I'm still a virgin, Uncle Jericho."

"You are," he snaps back as he continues to pressure me to put on that sad excuse for a dress.

"What, are you going to take me to the doctor's to verify this?" Sheltered as I am, I know there's no actual way to determine if someone is a virgin, but an asshole like my uncle probably still believes there is.

"We got ways of knowing, girl. Your buyer will know for sure. They're very experienced with girls' first times," he cackles, slapping my father on the shoulder when we get to him, and he laughs too.

"I can't believe you're doing this, Dad," I say, shaking my head.

"I need money, baby. And you're not exactly helping with the bills very much."

I grind my teeth. I'm his daughter. He's supposed to protect me. He's supposed to care for me. More than anything else right now, I feel terribly alone.

Uncle Jericho continues, "This is really the best you can hope for, Baylee. We're doing you a favor."

A favor? I can't even begin to understand my uncle's twisted logic.

I turned down some boys in high school. My self-esteem was never great – with relatives like these two, was it any mystery why? Anyway, I thought any interest guys showed was part of some cruel joke. I have learned a little better in the years since, I know my worth, and I never wanted to give myself to just any man. I wanted my first time to be with someone special — I want it to *count* somehow.

Now? It looks like I'm going to end up being given

to the highest bidder. Me and a bunch of other girls are about to be paraded out on stage like we are pieces of meat instead of living, breathing human beings. All of us eighteen, nineteen, twenty years old, that fact being fetishized by all these creeps here. It's enough to make a girl lose faith in all men forever.

Everything has been going so wrong in the past few years. My mother passed, and then my grandmother not too long after that. That's what sent my father down this dark path. It's what led him to fall into Uncle Jericho's bad influence. At least, that's what I told himself.

I fidget with the ring on my finger, a habit. It belonged to my grandmother, her wedding ring, and the one thing I have to remember her by. It's not a fancy ring, given that she was never a very rich woman, but that doesn't matter to me. Holding it fills me with memories of a better time. Of being ten years old and helping her in her little garden. She put so much pride into that little patch of dirt, and I did too. Raising vegetables and hoping they'd turn out nice and juicy. From the tomatoes she grew herself, she made the sweetest spaghetti sauce, always saying it was the product of all of our work together.

What would she think if she saw me now? Standing on a shoddy-looking stage in the dark, waiting for a bunch of disgusting old men to come out and throw money at the chance to deflower me. My first time, sold off to make Uncle Jericho a quick buck. He doesn't care if they're nice to me, he doesn't care if they are sweet or tender with me. All he cares about is himself, and I'm just an asset he conned my father into selling. All so that he can have some more money to buy another fix and keep my father drunk out of his mind.

Grandma always told me how important love was. That I would find a man some day and I'd want to give myself to him completely, and that would be the start of the best years of my life. This isn't it. This feels like it can only be the beginning of something truly awful.

My only hope of getting out of here in one piece is that hot biker who I saw following us out here. I mouthed 'help' to him and then he disappeared. Did he give up? Decide I wasn't worth it?

Is he waiting in the dark for his chance to bid on me?

I need a hero, someone who will ride in and save me from all this, but that's the stuff of movies and romance novels. That's not real life, and there aren't enough real-world heroes out there to save everyone who needs help.

Not tonight, anyway.

5

BLAZE

"WHAT'S THE STORY, BLAZE?" Scar asks as he rolls up next to me, keeping enough distance from the event so as not to give the presence of our bike armada away. "Why are you calling a sudden red alert?"

I run my hands through my hair. Why did I call them here? I don't know this girl. She isn't anyone to me. You don't call the Wildfire calvary in on just any problem.

This is a worthy problem, but I have to phrase it right. "They have my girl in there, Scar."

That's only half a lie. I guess it's a bit much to call her my girl, after all, I don't even know this woman's name. And she's married. But damn, I look at her and I feel like she's mine. Maybe I'm just going soft, maybe I'm going a bit crazy. But I'm worried about her, not to mention the sheer shady shit that's going down here.

All those girls need our help. I don't feel too bad about not being wholly truthful with Scar.

The club president raises an eyebrow. "Color me a little surprised, given this is a virgin auction."

I cock my eyebrow. "And you know that how?"

"Part of being president is knowing what's going down in your territory, Blaze. These fuckers have been doing this for a while."

"And you've allowed this bullshit to continue?"

Scar shakes his head. "Don't give me that look, man. You know how it is. I know it's bullshit too. But I can't be riding around being fucking Captain America every week. I've tried to run them out. I gave the pigs the tips to bring this operation down. Not surprised they fucking failed. Probably some of the buyers, knowing them shitheads. But you know how it is, Blaze. You know how dangerous it is to go to all-out war."

There's grumbling through the ranks. I don't doubt that Scar has the club's best interests at heart, but it doesn't mean I'm not infuriated hearing it.

"But," he continues, a smile coming to his face. "If they got your girl, they got one of us." He winks knowingly at me and adds, "Didn't know you had a girl, but that's enough for me to abandon being all prudent about turf wars and start making decisions about going and fucking some shit up."

I laugh. "That's the president I elected."

"Come on, boys. We got work to do. We don't stop until every girl in there walks free." He revs his cycle, and gets revs in return. "Although I'm going to suggest that Blaze hurry up and make his girl not a virgin so she don't end up in a place like this again."

More laughter, and I shake my head. I think on some level Scar knows I'm full of shit, but he's going along with it anyway.

First things first, we go out to do recon. We scope out the joint, and a few of us infiltrate the event. Not approaching as an army, but as potential customers. Luckily for us, tattooed musclebound dudes wearing a whole lot of leather aren't a rarity here, so we are able to hide in plain sight.

The 'show' starts. And I can see my girl in the wings. "Gentlemen, gentlemen," a sleezy man in a suit shouts out, no microphone because a shitty place like this doesn't exactly have a PA system. "Tonight we got some very special girls that you're all going to be happy to spend big bucks to have first-time exclusive access to!"

I grit my teeth, watching my girl in the shadows alongside the other women that are being treated as products to be bid on tonight. She's sobbing, tears streaming down her face, and the same can be said of the others. As much as I feel for the other girls, my focus is intensely on her.

"First up, we have the lovely and precocious

Sasha..." the faux-MC shouts, and some musclebound idiot drags the young woman onto the stage. What she's wearing can generously be called a dress, if you have no standards of decency whatsoever. She's bawling her eyes out. This Sasha may not be the object of my fascination, but she's going to endure a terrible fate if I stand by and do nothing. But I'm waiting for Scar's signal. "Do I hear ten thousand?"

"Ten thousand!" a voice next to me shouts out. It's some suit-wearing asshole. I glare at him. He looks at me. "What?"

I just stare, wishing my disapproval had the ability to kill.

"You think ten thousand is too much?" He follows my eyes to my girl in the wings and smirks. "Oh, damn, look at the knockers on that one. Maybe you're right, maybe I better save my money."

He's talking about my girl.

And it's enough to make me act without thinking, damn waiting for Scar's call.

My fist goes sailing right into this asshole's nose.

Security moves in, but my brothers are quick to act, striking them down too, using fists before guns. The bullet-free battle doesn't last forever though, as someone starts firing.

The entire event falls apart. The girls are screaming, as are some of the men. Most of the buyers are cowards, fleeing the scene at the first sign of conflict. I run toward the stage, toward my woman. She's looking right at me, her eyes wide and white, shocked at what she's seeing in front of her. I scoop her right up and over my shoulder and high-tail it out of the crowd. More than anything, I want to make sure she's safe.

The other girls are swept up too, my brothers taking my cue to get the innocents out of the line of fire before anything else goes wrong.

"Run, run, you motherfuckers!" Scar shouts as the chaos erupts around him, throwing punches along the way. "You're going to do this bullshit in my town, you're going to end up with assholes full of lead!"

I can't help but smile at his gusto. I'm proud to call him my president.

Once we're out of harm's way, I put my girl down, still utterly exasperated. "Who... who are you?" she stammers.

"The name's Blaze. And you may be married, but you're mine."

6

———

BAYLEE

THE BIKER IS HERE, and this hero is more real than I ever imagined. He helps me me onto the back of his motorcycle as I look at him in awe. He's a whole lot hotter up close, but the rushing in to rescue me from having my virtue sold off to some creepy old guy is likely coloring my opinion a bit.

Gunfire rings out from the crowd. Blaze climbs onto the bike. "I didn't go through all that to let you get hit with a random bullet. We're getting out of here, we can talk later."

With that, he revs the bike, and he peels out onto the road. Never having been on a motorcycle before, I wrap my arms around him in utter fear of falling off.

He's thick. Muscular, but also like a teddy bear in a way. Holding onto him fills me with a safety I haven't felt in quite some time. It's like whiplash compared to how incredibly vulnerable I felt mere minutes ago.

I'm being driven away from that whole cruel mess. Away from my father's sick whims, and the exploitation by Uncle Jericho. And unlike all the times I ran away alone, I don't think Blaze is going to allow them to drag me back again.

It's so weird. I have no reason to believe this so strongly. I barely know him. I had laid eyes on him in a couple moments of weakness, imagining him as some sort of hero figure. Yet here he is. Being that hero. The hero I need.

"Never got your name, sweetie. What do I call you?"

"Uh... I'm Baylee. With two Es," I say, realizing instantly how trivial spelling my name is at this moment. He could spell it Beileiy and I'd still be forever grateful for his help.

"Baylee, huh? Sweet name for a sweet girl."

We ride on the motorcycle for what seems like an hour, but when we get back to the very bar that I was dragged out of earlier tonight, I'm left wishing that the trip was even longer. I step off the bike, my legs aching and feeling like they can barely hold me up anymore, and yet I don't want to let go of him.

"Why are we back here? Did you drive all this way just to take me back to the bar?"

"Did you have somewhere you wanted me to take you instead? A family perhaps?"

I shake my head. "No. No, please, the last thing I want you to do is to take me back to my family."

He laughs. "Then you'll come and meet my family instead."

"Your family?"

We walk slowly to the bar, and right behind us a row of other bikes pull in. On the backs of five of them are the other girls, as exasperated and exhausted as I am.

"The Wildfire MC became my family when my blood family was no more," Blaze says. "I trust them with my life, and I can count on them to help me do stupid shit like storm a virgin auction to rescue a pretty girl whose name I didn't even know."

"They brought back all the girls from the auction?"

"Of course, we're not going to let anyone get hurt. We'll keep 'em all here until we figure out what all of you want to do next. Until then, you're safe here."

"At a bar?"

He laughs again. "This place is more than a bar, sweetie."

He guides me around the side of the bar to the back that opens to a whole other building. I think the best word to describe it might be complex.

We go inside and down a hall, where he brings me to a fairly large bedroom, the window wide open. The heat of the summer air flows in and I take it in. I'm starting to calm down from everything that's happened and now I'm putting the pieces together. "This is your place?"

"Yep. All of the Wildfire MC members have a room here. Sometimes it's their only place. True for me, but I think this is a pretty nice little room I have."

I nod along. It's big enough for a big bed and closet, and has quite a nice view. It's definitely better than the little shithole that is my father's house.

Blaze puts one hand gently on my shoulder, like he doesn't want to hurt me, or scare me. "There's a bathroom through that door, complete with shower. You can wear my robe after, or look in my dresser for some clothes. Are you hungry?"

It's not until he mentions the word 'hungry' that my stomach growls and reminds me that yes, it has been quite a while since I've eaten anything.

"I'm going to take that as a yes."

Suddenly, I'm overcome with emotion, gratitude that this man rescued me. Relief that I'm away from my dad and Uncle Jericho. I throw myself into Blaze's arms and he returns the hug.

"You're safe now. No one is getting into our club and hurting anyone, Baylee."

"Thank you."

After a long moment, he parts, and I'm left alone in his room.

I walk toward the window and take a deep breath of the fresh air before my legs finally give out and I fall back onto the bed. I've got tears running down my cheeks. It has all been so overwhelming. But now that I am here, in Blaze's care, I really do feel safe. It has been so long since I hadn't lived in fear, but for all of it to come this quickly?

It'd leave anyone overwhelmed.

7

BLAZE

"WE GOT the pigs to come and clean up our mess," Scar says as he pours himself a cup of coffee. "Made sure the remaining girls were safe before clearing out. Wouldn't want them to think we were vigilantes or anything crazy like that."

"The remaining girls?"

"A few stayed behind, wanted to go with the cops, press charges and all that. Bout half a dozen came back with us — I think our boys had an eye for them. Like you did, Blaze."

I cross my arms. "I was after my girl, Scar."

"Yeah, your girl who you haven't slept with yet. Who I never heard of until tonight. I'm not calling any bullshit, Blaze, just saying some of the other guys caught similar feelings."

I throw my hands up, not admitting my crimes but

not needing to. "Hopefully none of them are too traumatized from all that. I highly doubt any of them were selling their virginity willingly."

"I'm just going to say I'm not going to feel bad for any of those poor suckers who got in the way of a bullet tonight."

I nod agreement. "No injuries in our club then?"

"Hawk bruised his hand punching some bastard too hard, but that's the worst of it."

"That's the most Hawk way he could have injured himself."

"Some bandages and some ice, and he'll be breaking his hand on someone else's skull in no time."

I nod along as I grab a bottle of water for Baylee. "I trust the boys will be on their best behavior with the girls."

"You know the rules, Blaze. We got a zero-tolerance policy for bullshit. Women are our wives, our sisters, our mothers, our daughters. Unless one is trying to murder you, you show the proper fucking respect."

I grunt. It's not just talk. We've kicked out a few guys who were caught battering their old ladies.

Water in hand, I swing by the kitchen to grab some food for both of us. Then I head back to my room.

I walk in to see Baylee fresh out of the shower, presently covered in my oversized robe, her hair wet and slick. Despite showing zero skin, I can't help but feel my cock swell a bit when I see her, knowing that her naked flesh is touching my robe. Is it too much to hope that maybe soon I'll be pressed against her flesh too?

"Brought us both a burger, and I got you onion rings. Figured the latter would feed you if you were a vegetarian or something."

"Oh, um, thank you," she says, smiling nervously at me. Even an uncertain one like that tickles me just right. "Right now I don't care about anything like that, I think I could eat an entire cow."

"Would like to see that," I chuckle. I place the bag of food on a small table. Greg, the club's chef, was busy when I went to see him. Seemed like a lot of the other guys had a similar idea about feeding their hungry new guests.

Cracking open the styrofoam, I'm greeted with the wonderful smell of what Greg prepared. It is bar food through and through, and sometimes that's exactly what you want. Thick, greasy, and filling, and I believe I worked up enough of an appetite to enjoy just that.

Baylee inhales the onion rings, nibbling on the burger. She's a lot hungrier than she let on, and sucks down the water too. I can't help but stare as she digs in.

She slows down, and looks my way, looking guilty and sexy as all hell. "Am I doing something wrong?"

I laugh. "No. I'm just glad to see a girl with an appetite. I like it."

She smiles. I'm already addicted to the sight of it.

I join her in enjoying the food, although I have big,

thick steak fries instead of the onion rings I got her. I look at that ring on her finger, its gold glinting in my eye. "Where's your husband in all of this?"

She freezes, and looks at me with her eyebrow cocked. "My husband? What do you mean?"

"Your husband. He surely should have stepped in during this whole terrifying situation." I'm struck with a huge dose of dread. "No. He couldn't have been the one who put you in such a situation, could he?"

"I don't have a husband," she says, shaking her head. "And I don't know why you keep saying I do."

"Your ring. Isn't it a wedding ring?"

She looks at the ring on her finger. "This?"

"Doesn't look like costume jewelry to me, though I'm no expert on fashion." I've been in nothing but leather and denim for the past five years of my life, never worn a piece of jewelry in my life, so I'm not about to give anyone, let alone a lovely woman, anything resembling a jewelry appraisal.

She shakes her head. "Oh no. No, it's not like that at all! I'm not married."

"Ring sends that signal, you know."

It dawns on her as I say the words. "That's what it says, doesn't it?"

"Yeah. Any guy who shows the slightest bit of respect for a woman won't go after her when she's got a ring like that. Says she's already married and no one likes a homewrecker."

She fidgets with it. "I guess that's why I haven't had too many guys approach me. I thought that was a bit weird."

"No Wildfire man wants to get involved with a married woman."

Baylee chuckles. "I guess so."

"So what's the story then?" I have to say I'm very relieved to hear that she's not married. To an embarrassing extent. It makes me feel like some sort of selfish asshole, when I'm sure the last thing she wants after tonight is someone a decade older than her creeping on her again.

"This is my grandmother's ring. It's all I have to remember her by."

I sigh. "And you hold her very dear, I'd suppose."

She nods. "She was the sweetest and kindest person in the world. When she was alive it was the last time I was ever truly happy."

"I'm sorry to hear that it's been so tough for you, girl."

"It's not your fault."

"It's not. But I'm so glad to hear that you're not married. No boyfriend either?"

She shakes her head. "No. Why? Why are you so concerned with my relationship status?"

"Because the moment I saw you at the bar tonight, I realized that there's nothing more that I want than to make you mine."

She turns beet red. She stands up and approaches me, placing a light hand on my shoulder. "I don't know what to say to that... But I do have to tell you — thank you, Blaze. Thank you for saving me."

I laugh back at her with a smile. "Girl, I think you're the one saving me."

She looks my way, those big brown innocent eyes of hers staring right at me and leaving my heart skipping beats.

Then, showing some fire in her belly, she makes a move. She leans in, and plants a kiss right on me.

Her lips on mine are beautiful and electric. My mind is racing and I'm in heaven.

Fuck.

She's too good to be true, and yet? She's right here. Wanting me. Desiring me.

And I can't wait for what she'll do next.

8

BAYLEE

I DON'T KNOW what I'm doing.

Kissing a man I have just met isn't how I usually do things. I've had dates before, but I usually am very reserved. Hand-holding seemed like a bridge too far for me in those cases.

Now I have my lips on his, and I'm wearing nothing more than a bathrobe. His bathrobe, no less.

But it feels right all the same. I'm not kissing him just because he happens to be my knight in shining armor, riding in at the last moment to save me from the clutches of some disgusting villain. No, I'm kissing him because he makes me feel something I haven't felt before. That I am more than some small-town girl, that I'm not just some asset to be bought and sold. He looks at me like I'm a woman, like I'm loved, and that maybe, just maybe, everything will be fine.

Which may be too rash. I break the kiss, blushing as I stagger away from him, sit down and nervously nibble on an onion ring.

He's overwhelmed. He shakes his head, looking like he doesn't know what's happening. Did I go too far? Maybe he's just a nice guy and doesn't find me attractive? How unfortunate that would be, but it doesn't change that I appreciate what he did for me.

He strokes his stubble. "Uh... so, what happened tonight? How did you end up at a virgin auction? The club was making the safe assumption that neither you nor the other girls were there out of their own free will."

"No. I didn't want to be there. I was only there because my Uncle Jericho and my dad forced me to go there, saying they'd kick me out on the street if I didn't go along with it."

"Your dad? Your own father made you go up on stage to sell your virginity?"

I nod. "I want to believe he's been corrupted by my uncle, but he still allowed this all to happen. I don't think I can trust and love him anymore. The man who I once knew has been gone ever since my mother and grandmother passed."

He grunts, angry. "I'm sorry that happened. That's absolutely horrible and I wouldn't even call that man your father anymore."

"It's hard to swallow, but you're probably right."

"You're welcome to stay at this club as long as you want, so don't take this as a plea for you to figure it out, but do you have anywhere to go? I doubt you want to go back to that man, and I'm not sure I could let you go if you did want to."

I shake my head furiously. "No. Heavens no! I don't think I can ever feel safe around him again after tonight."

"And you feel safe with some random biker dude?"

I giggle. "Yes. It's crazy to me, but in the brief time I've known you, you've shown me more kindness than I've experienced in years."

He smiles for a moment before it collapses. "It's awful you had to come here just to get that."

"It's fine. I think it'll all work out as long as I'm here with you." I lick my lips, the butterflies inside me kicking into high gear. I can't believe I just said that out loud, and yet I'm feeling frisky every time I look at him, acting in ways that I never envisioned myself acting.

"I don't want to put you in a situation where you traded one asshole for another, Baylee," he says, unable to take his eyes off me. "I'm not requiring any sort of payment for my kindness."

An honorable man and a sweetheart. "I know it's not transactional, Blaze. My heart is aflutter seeing you, a sweet man who will go against my uncle without anything personal to gain. One who's so handsome on top of that. You're everything I could ever want in a man." I want to wrap my arms around him. When I held him riding back from the auction, it felt so right to be so close to him. And I want to feel that way again.

He's the kind of guy I want my first time to be with. Someone I won't regret giving myself to. Because they just may be the only man I'm ever with.

"You keep talking like this, Baylee, you keep approaching me, keep bending over in that robe and getting dangerously close to letting yourself spill out of it... you're going to find out what I'm holding back, little girl. How bad I want you. How bad I need you."

I saunter over to him, much in the way he just warned me against doing. Maybe with even more of a risk of having myself spill out of the robe. "How bad do you want me? How bad do you need me?"

"I could tell you, or maybe it's best I show you." He takes my hand, and guides it between his legs. I feel something hard and raging, something desperate to get out of its denim prison. "I want to do reckless things with you, Baylee. If you don't want me to hold myself back, you're going to have to want this as badly as I do."

"I want you, Blaze. I want every bit of you."

"I want to throw you down on my bed, strip you bare. I want to put my lips on your clit, lick and suck it until you're screaming for me. I want to squeeze your tits in my hands, watch you shudder as I show you so many sensations you haven't felt before. Then I'm going to spread your legs when you're all nice and wet for me, and I'm going to be your first. I'll be kind, I'll be sweet, and I'll be gentle, just long enough for you to get used to it. Then I'm going to fuck you, Baylee. Good and hard. Until I make you scream for me, until you're begging me to do it again and again. And I'll do it gladly. I'll keep you a naked, quivering mess of orgasmic flesh on my bed, happily coming for the rest of your days."

His words are dirty, and I already feel my own heat raging. It's what I want. What I need. I may be an innocent virgin, but I am also a woman with desires. Who wants to be loved, to be cared for, and Blaze is who I want to be loved by. I shrug the robe off me, letting it drop to the floor, revealing my completely naked body before him. His eyes roll up and down my form, he's licking his lips. I wrap my arms around his neck and look him dead in the eyes. "Don't tell me those things, Blaze. Show me them."

He growls, taking me right off my feet, his hands caressing my ass as he carries me to his bed, planting me flat on my back.

I can't wait for what is going to come next.

9

———

BLAZE

I'm amazed at how hungry she is for me. It makes her all the sexier.

A real man doesn't want his girl to be a passive waif in her lust. Someone who's only a vessel for his release. No, a real man wants a woman, one who is as fiery and hungry for sex as he is.

After everything that went down, I expected that the last thing on Baylee's mind would be any sort of sensuality. That perhaps she would grow to hate her body instead of viewing it as part of her that should be embraced.

I'm so glad to be wrong. She's beautiful, and I run my hand through her drying hair, appreciating what's in front of me. Her tits are gorgeous, her cunt is calling to me, but damn, I have to hold myself back. She's a virgin, after all. I'm an enlightened enough guy to know that it doesn't have to hurt, she just needs to be good and ready. She deserves someone who's going to take his time, make it feel good for her, not some idiot teenager slamming in there like a drunkard with a set of keys.

I pull my shirt off, and she's quick to run those dainty hands down my chest, making me purr with excitement. She enjoys my body as much as I'm enjoying hers. I steal a kiss from her, and she's so eager to share that with me. This time, our tongues meet and it's powerful. Her lips are candy and I can't get enough of her. The only thing stopping me from keeping it up is the allure of the rest of her body.

Kissing down her neck to her tits, I grab more than a handful of each. Those nipples of hers are perky and powerful, and I tickle them with my tongue, hearing her gasp and shiver at what I'm doing to her. I thought seeing her smile was the most beautiful thing, but hearing her moan for me is a strong competitor.

She runs her hands through my hair, her touch igniting such wonderful feelings within me. I show each of those tits the proper reverence before leaving them with an enduring touch as my lips go lower down her body. Enjoying every bit of her soft flesh as I close in on her sex.

I let my hands roam down, enjoying her thighs, her calves, and my eyes are focusing right on her pussy. It's already wet and inviting me, but I'm not going to let that fact deny her the joys I can give her that aren't just from my cock.

Her cunt is cute in itself, like the rest of her, but how she's offering it to me is so damn hot. I run my finger down her form toward that nub, touching it, watching as she jolts a bit, gasping in delight from what I'm doing. My touch only becomes firmer, tickling her harder. My fingers tickle her nub as they slide into her slit bit by bit. I keep a close eye on her, making sure there's never a wince of pain in her eyes. She told me she feels safe with me, and I'm not about to exploit that trust.

I kiss her again, between her thighs this time. She tastes so damn sweet, and I slurp her juices, watching as she gasps and writhes as I take her in and keep up my worship of her. My tongue slides into her, and I lap up her juices. A jolt of lightning tears through her and her hands go right for my head, grabbing handfuls of my hair.

I nuzzle against Baylee, my whole face against her sex, and I can feel that she wants every little thing I do, every movement I make, all of it to stimulate her, all of it to make sure that her first time will be memorable for all the right reasons. I will be the opposite of whatever bastard hoped to buy her instead of earning her trust.

She struggles against me. Inexperienced, but she's still a woman has an idea of what she wants. She's rubbing her clit as I eat her out, my tongue fucking her and taking her pleasure her higher. Knowing she's liking every bit of it, I pick up the pace, slurping her juices dry only for her to be so aroused by me that they instantly return.

The fire inside her is roaring as she screams out for me. I'm addicted to the sounds of her pleasure, to the taste of her cunt, to everything about her. All it took was one hit and I'm absolutely hooked on her.

I feel her against me when she comes. Her legs cross around my head, her muscles convulsing, all of her throbbing with such strong and absolute need for what's happening. I won't stop. I want her to fully enjoy anything and everything that I'm doing to her, to be as addicted to me as I am to her.

She's the orgasmic puddle of flesh on my bed that I promised she'd be, but she's young and the fire of her libido will not be quenched for long. She pushes herself up, giving me the most powerful 'fuck me' eyes that I've ever witnessed.

"Pants off," she demands, and it's a wish I'm happy to fulfill.

I unbuckle my jeans and lower them, along with my boxers, shoving them right down my legs. Her eyes go wide as she sees my cock spring out, throbbing hard, now unrestrained. It feels damn good to let it fly free, and the pride comes strong when she stares at me with absolute awe in her eyes. She's a modern girl. She has the internet. She knows what a cock looks like, and has likely seen them before. Yet she looks at me like I'm greeting her with some monstrous behemoth. I can't help but laugh.

"I need to taste more of you, Baylee. But I know your desires won't let this be a one-way street." I lie down next to her. "Sit on my face, girl, and do what comes naturally to you."

She nods, still very meek about what's happening. She tosses her leg over me, and brings her pussy down to my face. Then she grabs my cock, and I feel a throb of delight shoot right through me.

Damn, this girl is going to be a test of my stamina.

10

BAYLEE

IN THE TIMES when I've explored my own body, I never felt nearly as good as I do when Blaze first put his lips on my pussy. And here he is, doing it again, not even ten minutes after the first time.

I'm more than ready for it, but I don't want him to be doing all the giving. I eyeball that monster of a cock that's pointing straight up at the ceiling and realize the way he positioned us, I can give as well as receive when it comes to pleasing one another. I stroke him, building up confidence in what I want to do.

I hear him laugh at my timidness, but it only emboldens me. I run my fingers down to his balls, seeing they are heavy and hot for me, so ready to explode, just waiting for me to do the proper thing and give him a reason to come for me. My grip is light but firm, I run my hands down his length as I bring my lips to the head of his cock and kiss it.

Only to gasp as Blaze licks my nub, sending another blissful bolt of lightning right through me.

I won't be stopped though. I lick the head of his cock, and run it down his length, hearing his low groans from my touch. I wriggle against his pokes and prods with his fingers and tongue, aching to give my own. I stare the cock down, building myself up, wondering how on Earth that thing is going to fit inside me, be it my mouth or my pussy, let alone anywhere else.

My mouth opens wide though, and I meet him, sliding that length into my mouth, taking in the musky scent and the manly taste of him. Deeper and deeper, my hand is still around his cock as I guide it into my throat, until it feels like I can't take any more of it.

"God, you just keep surprising me, Baylee. Your mouth is a little slice of heaven."

I chuckle around him before stroking him and sliding his cock out of my mouth, licking up his length before taking him in again. His groan is long and powerful and I quite enjoy how he sings my praises. All the while he keeps a slow and steady focus on my clit and my pussy, making my own pleasure hum through me as I try to suck him good and hard.

Feeling my body pressed against his is so powerful as he tastes me. This feels so right, like what love really is. Passion made physical, lust pushing us forward, knowing that we want to take care of one another even outside the heights of ecstasy.

We set a good rhythm as I bob up and down on his cock, his tongue penetrating me in much the same way. I'm gasping and writhing against his mouth, focusing even as an orgasm starts to wrack me again, making it feel like I can't do anything else. But I'm driven. I want Blaze to enjoy every bit of bliss that I'm enjoying, and I won't stop until his balls are empty.

But by God, it's so hard. He's so good, and all I have is my eagerness and determination. If this wasn't my first rodeo, maybe I could manage it a bit better, but for now, all I have is my drive to please.

Sometimes, though, that's enough.

His groans become longer, more frantic, stronger, just as my moans around his cock do. Maybe as another point of evidence that we're perfect for one another, it feels like we come at the exact same time. His cock throbbing inside my mouth, his seed rushing through it, the heat of it blasting into my mouth. All so fast, all so sudden, all while I'm coping with my own orgasm.

How it's slamming through me, pulsing so hard, my body so sensitive to what I experienced so shortly before. I'm screaming out, muffled by his cock, the vibrations of my voice shuddering around him. It feels so good, with an added layer of sinfulness given what

I'm experiencing right at this moment. Him eating me as I suck him. And to think, I'm still technically a virgin.

Not that I will be for much longer.

The results of our lust for one another are quite messy. He came so much that it's far too much for me to swallow, his juices dripping down my chin.

He doesn't get away unmarked either. Blaze is laughing as he rolls away from me. "You're a squirter."

I panic. "What?" I look at him and he's drenched. "Oh, I'm so sorry, I didn't mean to..." I finally meet a hot guy, someone worth falling in love with, and then I go and do this to him. Just my luck.

He shakes his head. "No, no. I like that. Just proof of how good I ate you out. You're a special one, Baylee. I don't think I can get enough of you."

Blaze grabs a couple washcloths from the bathroom, wiping my chin and cleaning himself up as well. It's sweet and tender, a huge contrast to the whirlwind of lust we just enjoyed.

"You're so beautiful, Baylee. Even with my come all over your face, you're the hottest thing I could ever imagine. Maybe because of that." As we sit on the edge of his bed, he kisses me, running his hands down my back, gooseflesh forming at his mere touch. His kisses go further down my body. I know men can't come multiple times so easily, and that the two orgasms I have already enjoyed are one of the many gifts of womanhood.

He brings his lips to my tits, and suckles them, the good ache throbbing through me as he does so. Despite me supposedly sucking him dry, I watch as Blaze's cock twitches and comes back to life, as hard as it was when he first saw me. "You're... you're ready to go again," I say, a little bit intimidated.

"How many times do I have to tell you? You're really something special, Baylee. Are you still ready for more?"

Two wonderful orgasms already, and yet I'm still a virgin. I look Blaze right in the eye and nod. "Take me, Blaze. Fuck me properly. Be my first."

"You have no idea how much that turns me on," he says, meeting my gaze. "Not just that I get to be your first — that you chose me."

Back down on the bed, he crawls over me, kissing me face to face again, and I can taste myself on his lips. His cock throbs against my thigh, moving up to my abdomen, and it still seems so intimidating. As much as I want him, I can't deny that there's a bit of hesitancy. My father tried to scare me away from sleeping with boys by telling me how horrible it would be. I grit my teeth, grumbling, realizing he was telling me that so he could sell my virginity later, but it's beside the point.

I know it can be bad with the wrong guy. Blaze has

proved himself again and again to be the right guy. A kind, caring lover, a kind, caring man. The kind of man my grandfather was to my grandmother.

I reach between us, and wrap my hands around his cock. I guide him toward my slit, looking him in the eye, showing him my enthusiasm. His cock tickles my clit as he passes over it, inching toward my slit. The immenseness of his cockhead spreads my pussy. All the while, he keeps a watchful, caring gaze on me. He's not going to hurt me, I remind myself. He'll never hurt me.

His cock pushes into me. It feels so powerful, so immense. I gasp as he goes deeper, worrying that maybe I can't take him. But it's a stupid worry, as my body is so wet, so dripping hot and ready to accept him and everything he can give me. Soon enough, I accept all of him, and the bliss throbs through me, bringing a smile to my face. I never had anything to worry about when it came to Blaze.

He keeps a careful eye on me, making sure he doesn't do anything that would cause me harm. Steady, he withdraws, only to come back into me again, my body shaking with pleasure.

"Does that feel okay?" he asks.

My smile only grows, as does his. "It feels amazing."

I'm getting into it, squirming against him as our tryst becomes more fervent, more intense. I'm so wet for him, my cunt so hot, that my status as a virgin becomes irrelevant quickly.

It's not long before I'm turning into a slut, and more importantly, his slut. I'm crying out in pleasure as I buck into him again and again. He kisses me as he fucks me, bringing a sweet tenderness to the intensity of our lust.

"I love the way you shudder as I fuck you. How you squeeze my cock, how you moan for me…" He whispers into my ear, his breath intense and hot.

"I love… just about everything about you. Keep going. Fuck me, Blaze. Give me everything you got. Make me your woman."

We share another tender kiss as he does just that. He folds my leg against me, and brings his rough finger against my clit to rub me as he takes me again and again. We're so much closer now, so entwined, almost as if at this moment we are one being enjoying this to the fullest. Our bodies pulse with lust and with need. His arms wrap around me, my legs around him, his fingers combing through my hair. It's all so powerful and wonderful.

The pressure inside me builds and builds, my entire body shaking, moaning louder, faster. Every thrust builds me higher and brings me such wonderful joy, and I'm fully consumed by him. I scream out in orgasm for the third time tonight, my body throbbing as I fall back, a huge smile on my face.

Blaze is right there with me, his body so tense before he groans and releases into me, his own smile growing wider as he enjoys me. "So absolutely beautiful, girl."

"You're beautiful too," I whisper, my mind warped by pleasure and not realizing how awkward my compliment is.

He just laughs, holding me closer in his arms as he slips out, holding me as I begin to drift off, and I'm sure he's not far behind me.

Blaze has turned my life around so wonderfully in mere hours. He seems too good to be true. It couldn't all go this easily for me, could it? There has to be a catch.

There's always a catch.

11

BLAZE

I YAWN, stretching myself out. It's a beautiful day.

Not because of the weather. It's kinda gray and miserable outside, but sunshine itself is right next to me.

She tumbled out of my arms at some point last night, and is on her side, sleeping peacefully. I can't keep my eyes off her. Her being so forward with me took her from gorgeous to absolute perfection. I caress her hair, enjoying her softness. I lean in and plant a kiss right on her.

She giggles, her eyes opening.

"Go back to sleep, I was having so much fun just watching you."

She shakes her head, her smile growing. "That sounds incredibly creepy, you know."

"I didn't mean it to, but you're just that beautiful, babe."

Ambition strikes her, and she leaps into action, pushing me down on my back as she straddles me, her beautiful, naked form swaying as she moves. She reaches down behind her, taking hold of my cock, already hard merely from lying next to her, now turned to steel at the way she's straddling me. Her tender touch is wonderful as she flashes me the most devious glare. "You fucked me so good last night, and all I did while I was asleep was dream about getting fucked by you again, Blaze. So if we're already here and naked..."

"I'm not complaining," I say as I place my hands on her hips and run them up her sides.

She flops down to kiss me on the lips again before guiding my cock toward her cunt, letting its heat envelope me so magically. I groan with bliss as she takes all of me, the intensity overwhelming. I massage her tits as she begins to ride me, her eagerness so infectious. She shudders so easily from my cock, and soon my hands settle on her hips as I help her along with my strength.

The rapid nature of it all sends a shiver down her spine and we only go at it stronger. We're enraptured by one another, the movements coming slowly, matching the pace of our fucking, my finger sliding down to her clit, rubbing it with every bounce she makes on my cock. Hearing her moans emboldens me as I start to help her. Soon she's slamming into me, both of us driven with a desire to see the other come.

And come we do. It hits us both at the exact same moment. She screams for me, in a way I'm sure is echoing through the rest of the clubhouse. I don't care. I want them to hear how much my girl loves me, and just what I'm doing to her. She has nothing to be embarrassed about.

I'm right there with her though. As she's taken by it, the deep, thudding orgasm hits me too, the rush of bliss through my core and into her so damn impressive. I never knew being with a woman could feel so damn good. I shoot my seed into her, her body so happily taking me, all of me. We are in perfect harmony with one another at that moment, the closest two people can ever be to becoming one.

She collapses on top of me, her hair whipping across my face. It's messy, but I want it no other way. I run my hand through it, and plant another kiss on her lips. I barely know this girl, but it doesn't matter. I'm madly in love and I will die for her.

For a time, we just lie there and enjoy the presence of another. In a perfect world, we'd just keep doing that. We'd probably fuck again after a few minutes. This world isn't perfect, though, even if with Baylee by my side it's turning out to be pretty damn good.

"Got some business to do today, girl."

"Hmm?" She slides off me, and I caress her.

"Work."

She traces a finger over my pec. "I thought you worked here. That you're a biker or something."

"That isn't a job. That's a brotherhood."

"What do you do then?"

"I run a garage with one of my Wildfire brothers. Work on bikes. Cars too, can't be a snob. Those family SUVs need repairs and they got money."

"So disdainful of the family vehicle, huh?" She cocks an eyebrow.

"I'm sure my tune will change when I have a family of my own. Can't exactly put you and the two-point-five kids on the back of my bike."

A laugh. "Already thinking of things like that, huh?"

"We aren't exactly using protection, now are we?"

She doesn't question me further. She hops off the bed and heads for the shower, and I'm tempted to follow her in there, but I got shit to do. If I go there with her, no one's gonna get clean and I'm going to be terribly late.

I take my turn, and come out to her wearing the shirt I was wearing last night. It's sexy as hell and seeing it makes me hard again. Edge will understand if I'm late, but I gotta take care of business — especially now that I have this angel to take care of too. Besides, the sooner I go, the sooner I can come home to her. "You're dressed I see, you want some coffee?"

"Coffee sounds lovely."

We head out to the kitchen and get our cups, and I provide her with plenty of cream and sugar packets to go with her coffee, but she takes it black. As if I could fall in love with her any more. We take our cups to the back porch of the club, a gorgeous fenced area where some of the members let their dogs run about.

"Wow," she says as she sits down in one of the straw chairs. "I wouldn't expect this back here."

"This is our home, Baylee. Business in the front, but uh... I guess it's not 'party in the back' since we party up front too, but it's home back here."

"I've been living in a tiny apartment with my father forever. We barely even have a back porch. It's like, a foot square of concrete and a guard rail."

"I've been in places like that. It's rough."

"This is lovely, though," she says, sipping her coffee.

"I figured until I got a family to call my own, this is a wonderful place to live. Got my brothers, got community. And I also got you now, babe."

She chuckles.

"When I have my own family, I'm gonna get a home of my own with my savings," I tell her. "The whole American Dream spiel. Home with a white picket fence and all that jazz."

"You have savings? Must be nice."

"What do you do, Baylee? Do you work?"

She nods. "I cook and clean for my father and uncle. I work part-time at a shitty little diner. Or I did. I'm never doing the former again, and the latter was just so I could have any money at all. Not a career or anything."

Life is tough here. I know the town is small and lacking in opportunity. It's probably why her father and uncle had so much sway over her. "Okay, what do you want to do? If you could do anything your heart desired?"

She sighs. "I'm not sure what I want. My plan was to save enough money to get out of this town, but beyond that? I was never sure."

"There's gotta be a dream in that head of yours. Your eyes shine too bright for there not to be."

She nods. "All I know is that I'd love to have a garden at some point. One like my grandma and I used to have. To grow some tomatoes and make the best spaghetti sauce for those I love."

I cackle. "I'd love to try some of that. I think we can make that happen. Here, even. Get you your own plot of land... until we get a place of our own and you have even more space."

I smile at her, and she smiles back. We haven't even known one another for twenty-four hours yet and we are already madly in love with one another. The stars have aligned for me, and it's about damn time. I enjoy my time with her, sipping coffee, an arm over her shoulder, knowing that it can't last forever, but I'm going to relish it all the same.

The back door to the club opens and another pair came out. It's Edge, tall with a shaggy beard, and there's a young blonde beside him. She looks familiar, and it takes me a moment to realize she's one of the girls we pulled from the auction last night. She had similar ideas about clothes as Baylee — she's wearing one of Edge's t-shirts. It's a good look, and a sexy one too. Looks better on my girl, though, if you ask me.

"I see I'm not the only one who didn't sleep alone last night," I say as he sits down, coffee in hand.

"Tara's very grateful for us showing up last night," he says. "I keep telling her I was just doing what was right. Finding her was a bonus."

"Isn't like that," Tara says. "I like you, Edge. You are a bit rough but you know how to treat a girl. I've figured that out good and quick."

Baylee giggles. "I'm just glad to see last night didn't turn out as awful as it could have for all of us girls. That was so cruel. I'm saddened that stuff can happen."

"Shitty world sometimes," I muse. "But we find the good parts and cherish them. I found my good part and she's in my arms now."

Baylee snuggles against me. It's nice being out here

with a friend and his girl. It's a bit saccharine, but saccharine can be pretty damn good sometimes. Plus, if Edge is here, I don't have to worry about him getting pissed that I'm not at the garage yet.

"I talked to Scar," Edge says as he finishes his coffee. "You two are welcome to hang around here as long as you want. You're our guests. Debbie will help you get some clothes even, you don't have to wear our t-shirts, as sexy as you look in them."

I look Baylee up and down, slowly letting my gaze roll over her legs. "Very sexy indeed."

"Blaze and I gotta head into the shop and fiddle with our wrenches for a few hours. As much as I think you two might like to see that, I bet you both need some time to unwind."

"A long bath sounds nice," Tara sighed. "I still feel dirty, and not the good kind of dirty either."

"That doesn't sound too bad," Baylee agrees. "I'll be waiting for you when you get back, Blaze."

The unspoken message dancing behind her eyes is, 'I'll be ready for you.' Damn, I want to unzip my pants and fuck her right here, audience be damned. Instead, I call on my iron will and pull myself up to stand.

I'm out of coffee and it's getting late. "We better get moving. You girls take care of yourselves, and let us know if we gotta break anybody else's ass for showing you two disrespect."

More laughter.

Edge and I head back into the club and toward the kitchen drop off our mugs. Once we're out of earshot of our ladies, I slap him on the back with a smile. "Amazing girls we got, don't we?"

"Hell yeah, brother. Hell yeah."

12

BAYLEE

FOR THE FIRST time in a long time, I'm living without an impending sense of dread. The fear that everything is going to go wrong, because I'm going to say something that'll make my drunken father flip out, or something that'd make Uncle Jericho needle me and destroy what little self-esteem I managed to build.

I don't feel that here. There's security here. Which makes me laugh. It's a biker bar with a biker clubhouse attached. It's full of the roughest people in the country, the type who tumble off a motorcycle going a hundred miles an hour, shrug, get back up and ride the same motorcycle again. The type of people who get into fist fights for fun.

The type of people who would raid a trafficking ring to save a bunch of girls being forced to sell their virginity.

I enjoy my bath. A guy like Blaze doesn't have the fanciest soap on hand, but Debbie, the 'old lady' of one of the elder members of the club, was there to provide me with something nicer, and some clean clothes. Such a sweet woman, you'd never expect that she is married to someone who's been in this club for forty years.

I can only stay in the tub so long before I prune up. I get out, and get dressed. A pair of jeans and a t-shirt to call my own. They don't fit perfectly, but I can't complain when they were found for me on such short notice. I go to the bar, and Tara's there enjoying some tacos. I chuckle at the absurdity of a place like this having a taco night.

"Hey, Baylee. You should get some of these, they're really good."

"I think I will, I'm pretty hungry." I wave to the cook, who nods. I realize then I have no money on me. "Uh... on second thought..."

He shakes his head. "Don't you even worry about paying, you two are guests of the club."

Tara smiles. "I could get used to this. A hot guy AND free tacos?"

"I'm glad to see you've gotten over what's happened."

"I'm not, I'm just really happy right now, trying to focus on the moment," she replies. "Still pissed that I was foolish enough to end up there."

"Your father set you up to sell your virginity too?"

Her jaw drops at that revelation, then she shakes her head. "Nah. There was a job offer to be a model. In this town. I should have known better, but I fucked up and wound up with a bag over my head the minute I mentioned I've never had a serious boyfriend."

I shudder. "Men."

"These men are pretty swell. Just the rest of the gender batting about.400 for me right now."

We chat for a while. About anything and everything, enjoying the tacos coming our way. She's a nice girl, and I'm happy to make a friend on top of everything else. We're not too sure what became of the other girls at the event, but they're in good hands if the Wildfire MC has anything to do with it.

Soon enough though, I'm left sitting at the bar, all alone. It's the afternoon, no one's in for the evening yet, and Tara went to take a nap. Said she wants to be nice and energetic for when Edge comes back home.

I sip some water and contemplate taking a nap myself, but remember that feeling of dread that I said I was happy to be without?

There is a reason I had it for so long. I was usually right to feel that way.

"Baylee. There you are. How fucking dare you run off like this?"

Uncle Jericho's voice. I turn in my seat to face the source. My scumbag of an uncle is there, flanked by my drunk-out-of-his mind father and some guy in a suit. He looks clean-cut, his hair slicked back, giving me real *American Psycho* vibes and looking woefully out of place inside this biker bar.

I freeze at the sight of Uncle Jericho. He stomps right up to me. "What are you doing here? You don't belong here, Baylee."

"Go away, Uncle Jericho. I'm not going with you ever again," I say, working up the courage to cross my arms defiantly.

"No, you're not going with me. You're going with him, Baylee." He gestures back at the suit behind him.

I glare with disgust toward the suit. "What? Why would I do that?"

"Because I paid a pretty penny for you," the suit says, "and I intend to collect what I paid for."

"The auction was cancelled, I never went onstage," I snap back.

"Yeah, but this man saw you waiting in the wings and he wants you," Jericho says. "He came right to us and offered to buy you outright, and your father agreed."

"Go with the man, Baylee," my dad slurs, barely able to stand on his own two feet.

"I like the cute, innocent types. They're the most fun to break," the suit says, adjusting his tie in a way that suggests he thinks it's cool and sexy to do that.

"No!" I yell. Some of the Wildfire bikers in the back

of the bar finally pick up on what's happening and suddenly they're surrounding us. Back-up. Thank god. "I'm not going anywhere, Uncle Jericho. Not with you, and not with this creep."

"That's funny," the suit says. "Because I've heard of this club and its... less than savory practices."

"Less than savory?" I glare. "They rescued us. From guys like you."

"Vigilantism is against the law, little girl. You can't just do stuff like that without police authority. And that's only the first of the charges I could get brought against this place. I have friends in very high places. Up to the Governor's mansion. I could have this whole building condemned from any slight code violation, and every person who calls this place home behind bars, waiting for a trial, no bail, for the countless charges that will be brought against them."

"Fuckin' lawyers," one of the bikers mutters.

"Victor Gabriel, District Attorney, nice to meet you all."

"Go fuck yourself!" another biker snarls.

"I'll fuck her instead, thank you very much." He clears his throat. "If one of your 'friends' here lays a finger on me, I'll destroy them with something far more powerful than muscles, little girl."

He's smugness incarnate. I hate him with all my heart, even more than I hate Uncle Jericho.

"So you're going to come with me. Quietly. I paid for you, and you're mine now."

I bite my lip as fear winds through me. The bikers are on edge. They don't care about his legal threats. They're about to act on pride and honor, as these types of men always do. They'll destroy themselves before they let me leave with him. And I can't let that happen to people who've been so nice to me, a complete stranger until yesterday. The only way to stop it is to cooperate with these assholes, as awful as that sounds to me.

I shake in place. I wonder if there's anything I can do beyond just going with this man. I wonder what Blaze would do, and I realize he'd have already throttled this Victor. And then I remember, last night changed one thing about me that has to be important to him.

"I'm not a virgin anymore." That's what this sick fuck is after, right? Some pure, untouched maiden he can claim as his own and deny the opportunity to experience another man?

What he says in response, though, surprises me. "I don't care."

"You... you don't care?" I cock an eyebrow.

"You think a shady operation like yesterday checks hymens or whatever? No. Whether you slept with a man or not has no bearing on anything to me. What I want is your innocence, little girl. I want to break you. I want you to cry for me. To scream for me. Oh, the things we'll experience together. They'll be so wonderful." He grabs me by the hair. "Now come along. My payment to your uncle only clears once you're in my car."

I want to scream. I want to plead. I want every biker in here to tear him, my uncle, and even my father apart, limb from limb.

But I can't do that. I don't want anything bad to befall this club. The people that have only showed me kindness. The place that houses the men that Blaze calls his brothers. I remember all the other girls. The threats against them too, how Tara and so many others were rescued.

I never expected something as good as Blaze to happen to me. Maybe it's not meant to be more than just the one night we shared. If my pain keeps everyone else here's happiness going? It's a small sacrifice.

"Fine. I'll go."

Victor laughs. He yanks me down off the stool, and urges me toward the door. Uncle Jericho is incredibly pleased with himself, and my father is too drunk to even know what's going on.

I'm terrified of what this man has in store for me. If what he wants to do with me is even legal. For as much posturing he does as a lawyer, it's pretty clear he doesn't give a fuck about the law.

All I can think of as I'm marched out is Blaze.

I'm so sorry, Blaze. I'm so unbelievably sorry.

13

BLAZE

"THEY TOOK BAYLEE."

Scar's words don't seem real. I didn't want to believe them. It sounds like a sick joke, but Scar is too practical to be a joker.

"The fuck do you mean, Scar?" I'm quiet, breathing deeply. Edge and I had gotten done at the garage, coming back to the club only to find the bar closed and our club president sitting at a table deep in thought.

"Her asshole uncle and dad showed up with some lawyer. He spouted a bunch of legal threats that sounded real and would destroy Wildfire. We were about to jump him anyway, but Baylee agreed to go with him."

I pick up a chair. I throw it. It crashes against the wall, splintering. "Why didn't you act faster? I trusted you with her."

"We should have, Blaze. But you know me. I always think before I act. It's both a strength and a weakness."

Edge crosses his arms. "No point in letting Blaze destroy more furniture." He's infuriated right along with me, but Edge isn't the one with a nickname synonymous with fire. Just like Scar, he can think things through.

"We'll get her back, Blaze. That's not a maybe, that's a promise."

"How did they even know she was here? Who's the rat?"

Scar leans on his clenched hands. "She came back to the place they picked her up from last night. Doesn't take a genius to guess where she went after a bunch of bikers showed up to ruin their fun."

"Who told them she was here in the first place then? Baylee told me she came here to get away from them because she didn't think they'd be able to find her here."

"That's... that's a good question," Scar nods.

I glare around the bar. Every member of the club is there. Hawk, Echo, Zebra, there's not anyone missing, and I figure no one would be dumb enough to show his face here after betraying us all like this.

No. Wait, there is someone who isn't here. "Where's Capone?"

"The prospect? He was here a minute ago."

"Just stepped out. Said he was going to take a ride to clear his thoughts," Echo says.

Without another thought, I storm toward the club's garage. Capone is there, helmet in hand, climbing on his bike. He doesn't see me as I come and grab him by his pencil neck and slam him into the wall. "Where is she?"

"I don't know what you're talking about," he pleads.

"Where's Baylee?"

"I don't know!"

"You told her prick of an uncle she was here yesterday, didn't you?"

"What if I did?"

I clench his throat even tighter. "You're still talking with your old gang, aren't you? The one with connections to her uncle?"

He doesn't respond verbally, just gags for air, but his eyes tell me that he knows the jig is up.

"You're going to tell me where her uncle is now, or I'm going to keep squeezing your throat until you never need to breathe again."

He nods so I ease up. "I will, I will, just let me down."

I realize his feet aren't even touching the ground, I had him jacked up against the wall so hard. I drop him, and he collapses into a mess. I look behind me and see Edge and Scar in wait, swinging the keys to their bikes.

They were ready to ride with me as back-up, if I had any doubts.

I look down at our failed prospect as he coughs and gags for air. "You got two minutes to get us an address or I'm going back to strangling you, Capone."

———

THE ADDRESS CAPONE came up with takes us to an apartment block in the shitty part of downtown. Just where you expect to find scum of the earth such as Jericho Adams.

Edge, Scar, and I approach the door. We exchange glances. I'm ready to kick the thing down, but Edge throws up a finger. He knocks on the door. No answer. More knocking, then he clears his throat. "Got a pizza here," he announces. "Online order already paid for. Don't want to leave it on the ground, man. Let me hand it to you."

I then hear shuffling from behind the door, Edge stepping aside. The door opens. "You're so late, I hope you're not expecting a tip," Jericho says, before being interrupted by my fondness for choking people who infuriate me.

"Where's Baylee?" I demand, pinning him against the wall. I glance around the apartment. It's an utter mess. Discarded pizza boxes and Chinese food cartons everywhere, smelling of a weird combination of weed, alcohol, and tobacco.

"Who the hell are you?" His teeth are clenched, he is struggling. It's useless and just annoys me more than anything else.

"The man who actually loves her."

"Just tell him where she is, man," Scar comments from behind me. "He's not usually this violent. It's kinda scaring me, to be totally honest."

"Why would you love her?" Jericho spits. "She's a useless brat, not even very attractive. Four out of ten at best, I'm surprised that idiot paid so much for her."

I squeeze his throat. "Stop insulting her and start telling me useful things. I'm not in the mood for bull-shit, and if I can't have my woman, I'm fine with doing twenty-five to life."

"Fuck, okay, okay!" He squirms. "Victor Gabriel is who she's with. Took her to his penthouse downtown. There, I told you, let me go!"

"Victor Gabriel, I've heard that name before," Scar says, thinking aloud. "I got some phone calls to make. You got this, boys."

Edge nods as Scar leaves us.

I stare into Jericho's eyes. "You're no longer her uncle. You have no relation to her. I don't even want you to think about Baylee again. If I see you, if I hear about you being anywhere near her? Let's just say I'm going to be even rougher with you than I'm being now."

I throw him down to the ground. He scurries out the door, making his escape, Edge just shrugging as the rat squirms past him. As back-up, his job is turning out pretty boring today.

"You! You can't treat my brother like that!!" Another man starts to run up to me from deeper in the apartment, but he's too drunk to do a proper charge. I deduce who he is quick. Baylee has his eyes.

I strike him across the cheek and send him crashing to the ground.

He groans. I kneel down next to him. "You're her father. *Her father.*"

"Bay- Baylee?"

"Yes. Her. The girl you're supposed to care for. To protect. To raise. Not terrify, not disappoint. Or *sell*, for fuck's sake."

He groans and writhes in pain.

"Look, I'm not going to pretend that you haven't had hell in your life. You've lost your wife, your mother, and a whole lot more. That isn't an excuse to do what you did. Your daughter is beautiful and I love her, and for some reason, I think she still loves you, so I'm not going to threaten you in the same way I did your brother. But I don't want you to see her again until you're sober, and ready to beg for forgiveness for everything you've done. If I see you again and you're anywhere near this drunk? I'll... I'll... I don't know what I'll do, and that should scare you. Don't break her heart again."

More groans. I have no idea if he even heard what I told him. Maybe he'll find his way. It'll be a long journey, and not everyone who tries makes it. For Baylee's sake? I have to hope that he will.

My fists are clenched. I've never gotten this angry before. To taste love and have it taken from me has inspired such rage. I got my nickname for being a bit of a hothead, but this feels dangerous.

I need Baylee. More than anything.

"Scar's got some interesting notes," Edge says as I leave the tiny apartment. "We know where she is, Blaze. You can calm yourself, don't work yourself into a heart attack."

"I don't think calming down is an option until she's in my arms again. "

"You know what? I feel that. If it was Tara, I'd be the same warpath."

We go to our bikes, Scar already revving his, ready to go.

It's time to bust up the face of a pretty boy lawyer.

14

BAYLEE

I GUESS, objectively, this is a nice view. I'm high up in his penthouse, looking down at the city, thousands of people going about their lives down there. Maybe I shouldn't complain so much. He's rich, right? So many girls want to get attached to some rich guy for an easy life.

I pace back and forth. Victor is in the bathroom, preening himself. I contemplate making a run for it instead of accepting my spot in a gilded prison where he can do whatever weird things he wants to do with me. Part of the fun for him is doing what he wants with someone who doesn't want it done to them, and I'm equal parts terrified and horrified to find out just what that is.

But if I run now, Wildfire, and Blaze, will be in trouble. Victor's threat against the Wildfire MC is ever-looming, and I don't want to betray them. Not after the kindness they showed me.

Victor comes out of the bathroom, shirtless, a towel over his neck but still wearing khakis. He's surprisingly well-built, and if his personality wasn't absolute trash I guess someone could consider him handsome. Not me. I'm practically gagging at the idea of his hands on me.

In fact, I can't imagine liking anyone other than Blaze touching me ever again. He's who I want, the only one I want. He has things Victor could never have, even with all this money, and he's kind and sweet, and has more soul than this man will ever possess in his life.

"Why aren't you in the dress I gave you?" Victor looks at me, very cross with me. It's his default state.

"I didn't know I was supposed to put it on. I didn't think we were going anywhere."

"You need to look the part, Baylee. I want you to be my pure, innocent virgin."

The dress he gave me is not what I'd call my style. It's cut very short, white and frilly, looking like something you'd stick on a bridesmaid at a wedding.

"Put it on. Now. And let me watch."

I shudder as I walk over to the dresser where it lies. I pick it up, and dread taking off my clothes in front of this man. All I am to him is an object to fulfill his twisted fantasy.

"Put it on. Or I'll put it on you myself."

I lay it down, my hands going to hem of my t-shirt. I take a deep breath, trying to build up the courage to go through with this. I should just get it over with. Blaze won't know where to find me. I'm a sitting duck, completely at this asshole's mercy.

"Do I have to get the knife? Undress."

A chill goes down my spine, but I'm distracted by sudden pounding on the door of the penthouse.

"For the love of... of all the times to bother me." He storms toward it. "Go away, just leave whatever you're delivering at the door."

The knocking continues. I raise an eyebrow. It's a rough, fast knocking.

"Fuck off!" Victor yells.

The knocker doesn't get the message. Instead he knocks harder, and then he kicks the door in. It flies open.

It's Blaze. There's an incredible anger on his face, a righteous fury that's even frightening to me, even though I'm definitely not his target.

"Who the fuck are you?" Victor yells, before Blaze storms in and seizes him by the throat and slams him against the wall. There's a technique in the way he does it, one that suggests he's done this before.

"Your reckoning, you piece of shit," Blaze hisses.

From the door, two more leather-clad men enter. I recognize one from coffee on the back porch, but the older one is unfamiliar to me. He has a smile on his face, chuckling to himself.

"You're those bikers," Victor says, barely able to talk through the chokehold Blaze has him in. "You've just signed your own warrants, tomorrow every single one of you lowlifes will be in prison."

I stand back and watch. I'm not usually one for violence, but I'm also not going to disagree with choking out Victor, not with what I know about him.

"I doubt that," Blaze snaps back.

A worry hits me. That Blaze has come here recklessly. That my needing rescued yet again has driven him to a terrible mistake. We can't be together if he's in prison, after all.

"Simple-minded fool," Victor spits.

"He may well be," the older biker says. "But I can do the thinking for him."

"Who the fuck are you?"

"Scar, President of the Wildfire Motorcycle Club, nice to meet you, and no, I don't have a business card."

"President? Hah, that's precious."

Despite Victor's apparent muscles, he's not doing too hot getting out of Blaze's chokehold. He punches and kicks at him, but Blaze endures. Guess he focused too much on his glamour muscles.

"Victor Gabriel, you're a man with enough skeletons in your closet to build an army," Scar begins.

"There's so much dirt on you that I'm surprised your legal opponents haven't brought it up yet."

Victor grunts. "I'm just a better lawyer."

"I guess you are, because damn, man. It doesn't take long to find someone who doesn't like you, and for criminal reasons."

"Liars. And it's easy to prove them as such."

"Yeah, yeah. I know if one girl files a complaint against you, it's easy to swat away. Could just be some crazy bitch, right? But when enough start to complain, people start to question it. There's gotta be some fire producing this smoke, you know? And it turns out I can get in touch with a whole lot of these girls. All of them stepping forward together, a lot harder to swat away, now isn't it?"

Victor snarls. "No one will believe them. They're all whores."

Scar shakes his head, still beaming. "Did no one ever teach you how to talk about a lady? A shame, but I guess no one would mistake you for some sort of gentleman."

"I'm still not hearing anything to suggest why you all aren't prison-bound. People have survived worse than what you're planning to throw at me."

"All right, I'll cut to the chase. Your bookkeeping is sloppy as fuck, man. All your bribes, all your payoffs. It isn't hard to find them if you ask the right people the right questions."

"The hell are you talking about? I cover my tracks perfectly."

"Do you? Do you know every source you use? Maybe I know a guy who knows a guy who works in your department and can get some confidential paperwork released. And I can call in favors to make him violate the secrecy he swore to you. Tomorrow night, the news could be spouting about how corrupt the district attorney is. There's going to be so much outrage that the state won't be able to ignore the trouble you're causing. Even with all your ties? They'll throw you under the bus to save themselves."

The color drains from Victor's face. "You can't possibly have the information you claim to have."

"Wildfire has a lot of friends, too, Victor. Actual friends. Not just people we paid off. Can you really say the same? Are the people you trust with your secrets really that loyal?"

The lawyer squints. "What are you proposing?"

"We're going to take Baylee here. And you're not going to do shit about it. You try to destroy us and we'll destroy you right back. She's an awfully lovely girl, but are you going to give everything up for someone you barely care about?"

The lawyer grumbles, shaking his head. "Fine. Have it your way. Let me go and you can have the girl."

Blaze keeps his grip tight. He looks at me and smiles, and I can't help but smile back. He closes his eyes. Something is running through his head. "No, I got something else I'm demanding on top of her release."

"The hell else do you want? You got your slut..." The words make Blaze's eyes flame with anger.

"No more," Blaze says, his gaze locked on Victor. "No more girls for you. No more bringing innocent, unwilling young women into your home to do your awful things to, whatever those things are. If I ever see or hear of you with a woman who doesn't want to be here? To hell with our deal, I'm coming back here to finish the job I should do now."

The words are powerful, and dig right into Victor's head. Blaze throws Victor down to the ground, and he hits it coughing and gagging.

Blaze runs to me, and I run to him. Our arms lock in an embrace, and we go right for the kiss. It's cliche as hell, but there's nothing that I want to do more than embrace him right now. To have him hold me. Okay, there's more that I want to do with him, but not with an audience. It can wait until we're home.

"We'll keep in touch, Vic," Scar says. "Try not to make our little relationship any more complicated than it needs to be."

More grumbling from the lawyer.

"I'm never letting go of you again," Blaze says, kissing me on the forehead and running his fingers through my hair. "Never letting you out of my sight."

I giggle. My guardian angel, here to hold me and protect me. No matter what happens, I can count on him to come through. That one last moment of dread was terrifying, but it's over now.

"I love you, girl. I don't care if it's crazy to say it so soon, it's true. I love you with all of my heart."

I smile. "I have to say I love you too, Blaze. My lovely roughneck biker..."

"My hot wife."

"Jumping right to that, huh?"

"Are you disagreeing with my plans?"

"No, no, it's just that we are moving faster than I thought was typical. Just an observation, not a complaint."

We walk side by side, hand in hand, following his friends to the elevator. "Nothing typical about me, babe. So why are you surprised that this is any different? You're mine, and you'll always be mine. I don't see much point in dilly-dallying about that fact when we could be making it official."

I'd be ready to say yes if he popped the question right here and now. I'm feeling so much joy at this moment, and am amazed at the idea that it could last forever.

But if I've learned anything from Blaze showing up and rescuing me? It's that life is just full of surprises.

EPILOGUE
BAYLEE

ONE YEAR LATER

I'm utterly exhausted.

I shrug the strap of my dress back up as I set Clementine down to sleep. She's a little angel, but two-month-olds are a load of work. I know my peaceful time is short, and I'm juggling so much already.

Once Blaze and I got together, it didn't take long for our sexual appetites to have some consequences, no matter how wanted those consequences were. I was four months pregnant on the altar, but I was so in love that I didn't care. It hardly matched my childhood imagination of how my wedding would go. I didn't see myself falling for a rough-and-tumble biker either, so the surprises just kept coming.

His real name, for instance. It's Blake, but hardly

anybody calls him that, myself included. Blaze is a cool, badass biker name, and to all of his Wildfire brothers, it's as good as his legal name. I laughed when he told me how he picked it. It's the most low-effort biker name he could have picked, but apparently he was put on the spot to come up with something cool, said the first thing that came to mind, and it stuck. He's a bit of a hothead, in a good way, so it fits him too.

I smile as I walk through the hallway of our new home. A nice little two-story house with a huge back-yard we picked out together, since he didn't think a biker club was the place to raise a child. It gives me plenty of space for my gardening, and is a huge part of my current lack of energy. Between Clementine, Blaze, and my time spent knee-deep in the dirt, I'm surprised I'm still standing.

Life's been pretty peaceful, even if it is busy. My uncle wound up in prison after he tried to do another virgin auction. I had to testify about his exploitation and what he tried to make me do. Photographic evidence was leaked of some previous auctions, and his involvement was cemented because he was in the pictures. They seemed to be from about the height of a motorcycle, but I kept that observation to myself. Wild-fire doesn't want too much of a reputation for working with the cops.

And Victor? The little truce Scar and Blaze bargained for didn't last long, but it wasn't any of the

MC's doing. Victor's enemies caught up with him. He got indicted on corruption charges, and once again, additional evidence is turning up against him from an 'unknown' source.

My father, though? Things with him have been more complicated. Part of me looks at him as a victim like me, taken advantage of by his own brother. But understanding does not excuse what he did, or what he allowed to happen. I didn't invite him to my wedding, but I spotted him there anyway. He was trying to be incognito, but once Blaze and I realized it was him, he ran away, too ashamed to face me. Maybe someday I can forgive him. Someday we can heal. I just don't know if that day will come anytime soon.

I open my bedroom door now and immediately have Blaze's strong hands around my waist, planting a kiss on my lips. "Is she asleep?"

"Sleeping like a baby. Because she is one."

Blaze laughs, his kind gaze bringing a smile to my face. "You're so fucking beautiful, you know that?"

"You tell me every day."

"Because I don't want you to forget." He pushes the straps of my dress past my shoulders, and it drops to the floor.

I came in here expecting to fall right to sleep. I imagined I was too tired to do anything else.

But he has a way of inspiring extra energy within me. I can't resist him, and am always more than happy to help him rise to the occasion. A trail of clothes behind us, we're soon smooching on the bed, our naked forms entwining and wanting to enjoy one another so damn much. Feeling his cock pressing against my mound, the anticipation of what's to come fills me with such lust for him.

I look outside, ever so briefly. It's another hot summer night. Much like the first time I met him. Much like the first time he had me. It's the first summer of our marriage, and what will definitely be the first of many hot wife summers to come.

BONUS SCENE…

Right After the Virgin Auction … When Edge meets Tara for the first time…

CLICK HERE TO READ: https://dl.bookfunnel.com/boqfq8jlt7

MORE FILTHY DIRTY SUMMER!

READ THEM ALL!

Welcome to a filthy dirty summer! Drop it like it's hot with your 17 favorite instalove authors! Each stand-alone story delivers a scorching, fantasy-fueled romance! No need to pack a swimsuit—your kindle is all you need for a wet and wild summer!

ABOUT THE AUTHOR

Click HERE to grab a free steamy read from Frankie Love!

Frankie Love writes filthy-sweet stories about bad boys and mountain men.
Frankie is ridiculously in love with her own bearded

hottie, believes in love-at-first-sight, and happily-ever-afters. She also believes in the power of a quickie.

Find Frankie here:
www.frankielove.net